where the fairy tales go

where the fairy tales go

Hunter Writers Centre Inc.
Newcastle NSW 2300

Published by
Hunter Writers Centre inc.
hunterwriterscentre.org

ISBN-978-0-6453756-3-3

Cover design by HWC Publishing
Typesetting by Keighley Bradford
2023 Published by Hunter Writers Centre Inc.

Contents

Introduction

Hunter Writers Centre has a diverse group of members who share a passion for writing, whether they be poets or short story writers, novelists or playwrights, essayists or writers of non-fiction. Some of our members are extremely accomplished in their craft and some are just beginning as writers, learning how to shape their words into something meaningful and a joy to read. Our members' backgrounds are as diverse as their writing styles and they are broadly representative of the population of the Hunter Valley: members who live in the city of Newcastle, in the larger towns of the Valley, and in smaller communities and on farms as well. One of the joys of reading a collection such as this is being able to experience that level of diversity. Every reader will find their own favourites amongst the pieces collected here.

The last few years have been difficult for the members of Hunter Writers Centre, with many of our usual activities cancelled or moved to online-only events as the world coped with the COVID-19 pandemic. Whilst some of our members were able to embrace the use of technologies which were, for many of them, new ways of communicating and working with each other, many others found that the online sessions didn't work for them and that they missed the personal touch of being in the same room together. Despite the difficulties of the last couple of years, Hunter Writers Centre was successful in receiving funding to activate the lighthouse precinct at Nobbys-Whibayganba. We have had a lot of positive feedback from the creatives who have undertaken residencies in the cottages and from people whose work has been displayed in the exhibition space and sold in the arts store.

Some of the pieces in this anthology have been part of exhibitions at Lighthouse Arts where writers have been asked to write something inspired by the exhibition theme or a particular piece of visual art. Other works have been pieces submitted by members for our regular members' competitions run throughout the year.

I hope you enjoy this anthology and appreciate the richness and diversity of writing that we, at the Hunter Writers Centre, are privileged to read on a regular basis and congratulations to the writers whose work has been chosen. In one of his speeches, Richard Flanagan, that wonderful Tasmanian writer, said that the role of the writer is 'in one sense ... the very real struggle to keep words alive, to restore them to their proper meaning and necessary dignity as the means by which we divine truth.' There is a lot of truth to be found in the words in this book.

Glenn Stuart Beatty
Chairperson
Hunter Writers Centre 2023

Yinal and Ngirrinbai

Bronwyn Frost

It was a lovely warm day as Yinal and Ngirrinbai kicked **pinna** (sand) at each other as they **murraliko** (were running) along the **wombul** (beach). They were watching as their **Tunkarn** (mother) and **Biyungbai** (father) gathered food, some to eat now and some would be taken with them to the place they would **koiyong** (camp).

Some **Tunkarn** were diving deep under the waves collecting lobsters, others were on the rocks collecting **munbonkan** (rock oysters) and putting them into their **kinnun** (string bags).

Their **Biyungbai** were standing on the flat rocks with their **kullara** (fishing spears) catching **makoro** (fish).

The **Ngarongeen** (old women) were **yinbilliko** (kindling a fire) in the **koiyung** (fireplace) that they used the last time they were here with **kollai** (wood) that Yinal and Ngirrinbai had collected and brought to the **wombul**.

As the **makoro** and lobsters were caught they were brought to the **tirriki** (fire) **kimulliko** (to cook) and **ngiratimulliko** (to feed) everyone. The fishing stopped when the **konara** (family) were **kuttawaiko** (satisfied with food).

Yinal and Ngirrinbai almost missed eating this meal as they were so busy enjoying **murraliko** and **kurkulliko** (jumping) in the **pinna** and splashing in the waves.

It had been a long time since they had been to this place.

They had finally come down from the mountains, now the bad weather had passed. It was the time to camp between the **wombul** and the big river. At a place where the **mullubin** (fern) grew.

While they were living in the mountains they ate food from there. Which was good, but they **pirunkakilliko** (were glad) of the change, that moving to the coast would bring in what they were now able to eat.

Soon **Tunkarn** and **Biyungbai** started **kaipulliko** (to call out) to the **wonnai** (children). It was time to leave and move to the place where they would **koiyong** beside the river.

They **uwolliko** (walked) through the **pinna** hills and down toward the river. To a **koiyong** that had been used by this **konara** since time began.

Punnul (the sun) was almost **pillatoro** (setting) over the mountains when they reached the **koiyong**. Everyone in the **konara** knew what needed to be done to get the **koiyong** ready before **tokoi** (night) came. **Kollai** was gathered from nearby trees and soon **tiriki** was in the **koiyong**.

When the **koiyung** was ready the **munbonkan** were thrown into **pimpi** (the ashes) by **Tunkarn**. Yinarl and Ngirrinbai knew that when the **kulling** (shells) opened they were ready to scrape out of the **pimpi** and left to cool. They didn't like waiting too long in case they were grabbed by other **wonnai**. Everyone loved their **pulli** (salty) taste.

When the **koiyong** became quiet and the **warea** (little) **wonnai** were **ngarobo** (sleeping) the **konara yellawolliko** (sat on the ground) near the **koiyung**. Some would **wittilliko** (sing) stories of long ago. **Nguraki** (the wise one) would **wiyelliko** (to talk) of stories. The one tonight was about **Wybagamba** and the **moane** (the kangaroo) who lived there. Yinal and Ngirrinbai were afraid of that place, they would never go there.

Yinal **nakilliko** (observed, to watch) the **Biyungbai** hitting **tunnung** (stones) collected with other **tunnung**. He **nakilliko** them **murrinupuliko** (to sharpen) so they could use these **tunnung** as **kullingtielta** (a knife). Small fragments that were broken off fell onto the ground beside them. Yinal knew he would one day learn how to do that.

Ngirrinbai **nakilliko** the **Tunkarn** making their **kinnun**, she would learn to make these too as she grew older.

For this **konara** this was the rhythm of their lives for millennia, the river rose and went down again, sometimes sandhills shifted, but they lived their lives in their country and they both moved together at a gentle pace. Until the day a strange looking **murrinauwai** (a ship) was seen out in the ocean. It brought **Englandkal** (men belonging to England).

Everything changed in this place, **Mullubinba**.

The **Englandkal** cut down trees to build houses and buildings for themselves. Places that had always been home for this **konara**, they weren't welcome and not able to be used anymore. They had to move their **koiyong** further away from the familiar places they had always known.

Each day became harder for this **konara** as the food and places that had been theirs were taken from them with no thought of how they would survive.

These new people changed the shape of the river and other important features of the country, the **konara** began to feel like strangers in their own land. Some survived, many didn't as the invaders not only changed the **purrai** (earth/land), they brought **munni** (sickness) that had never been seen before!

Today, digging down deep in these places, evidence of the countless lives lived here for millennia can be found all around, if you know and care to look. Many lives have been lived on the banks of this river. It's all still here, even if there are big cement buildings on top of it.

In another thousand years when someone else comes to have a look, they will find this **koiyung** place and the pieces of stones and **kullung** left by Yinahl, Ngirrinbai and their **konara**.

Pin na	sand
Mur ra li ko	to run
Wom bul	beach
Tunkarn	mother
Bi yung bai	father
Ko i yong	camp
Mun bon kan	rock oysters
Kin nun	string bags women used
Kul la ra	fishing spears
Ma ko ro	fish
Nga ro nge en	old women
Yin bil li ko	kindle a fire
Ko i yung	fire
ko l lai	wood
Tir ri ki	fire flames
Kon a ra	family
Ki mul li ko	to cook
Ngi ra ti mul li ko	to feed
Kon ara	family
Kut ta wai ko	to be satisfied with food
Kur kul li ko	to jump
Mul lu bin	fern
Pi run ka kil li ko	to be glad
Kai pul li ko	to call out
Won nai	children

U wol li ko	to walk
Pun nul	the sun
Pil la to ro	to set —the sun—the moon
To ko i	night
Pim pi	ashes
Kul ling	shell
Pul li	salt
Wa re a	little
Nga ro bo	sleeping
Yel la wol li ko	sat on the ground
Wit til li ko	to sing
Ngu ra ki	the wise one
Wi yel li ko	to talk
Wy ba gam ba	Nobbys
Mo a ne	Kangaroo
Na kil li ko	to observe
Tun nung	stone
Mur rin u pu li ko	to sharpen
Kul ling ti el ta	a knife
Mur rin au wai	a ship
England kal	man from England
Mul lu bin ba	place where the fern grows Newcastle
Pur rai	earth/ land
Pur rai	sickness

Awabakal words from *An Australian Grammar: Comprehending the Principles and Natural Rules of the Language, as Spoken by the Aborigines in the Vicinity of Hunter's River, Lake Macquarie, &c. New South Wales* by Rev L.E Threlkeld. 1834. Used with the permission of Shane Frost, Awabakal Elder.

Stories and poems submitted in
response to the pandemic

House Arrest

Eve Gray

The house has been arrested
cautioned to stay within
doors not to do more
than look out of windows
remain within the confines
of walls and the perimeter
of fences. These orders stand
for an unspecified period.

Faces pressed against glass
peer in prying geraniums trying
to hide their curiosity behind
coarse furred parasols,
blushing for the breath they leave
fugging up the window panes.

They are standing at ease
but on guard nevertheless.
The place is under house arrest
it must not leave the precinct
without an armed guard
and permission formed in triplicate.

Lawns cower mown down
beaten back by bullets of old rain
Inhuman voices patrol in gutter
and sluice the milk of inhuman kindness

below ground where it is no longer
relevant. The house in question
soon learns its walls intimately
all ceilings seen flawed floors
all known finger-printed into memory

There is nothing to do but wait
and measure the length of days
along halls take stock of dimensions
and the condition of the paintwork.
The house is under arrest
and I have been appointed gaoler.

The fourth horseman of the apocalypse

John Tierney

It made my Irish blood run cold. Standing in the fresh food people's vegetable aisle, I couldn't believe my eyes. The shelf was empty. This made the great toilet paper heist of March 2020 fade into insignificance. A real crisis was upon Australia. No spuds! The need for potatoes springs from deep in my Celtic DNA. Immediately, graphic images filled my mind of my great-great-grandparents' flight from Ireland, when the potato crops failed in the 1850s. If Australia cannot even produce enough potatoes to feed itself in 2020, I suddenly realised, we were done for!

At the time, I was on a 'sensible restocking' run (which is good). This is not to be confused with panic buying (which is bad). The latter behaviour could even bring on another tongue lashing from Sco-mo. 'Just stop it,' he intoned on one morning news bulletin, 'it is un-Australian.' Whatever that is. We kept our excursions out into Coronavirus land a secret from our six children who were becoming increasingly concerned about the welfare of their 'ageing' parents during the pandemic.

I had only been home for five minutes when there was a knock on our door. It was Amanda who lived in the apartment across the corridor. She often dropped in, usually to wait for the locksmith to yet again let her in. The conversation this time started on a positive note. She asked if we needed anything from the shops (code for toilet paper). 'No, we are fine,' I said gratefully.

Then the conversation took a more sinister turn. The hairs on the back of my neck began to rise as she announced the pending arrival of the fourth horseman of the apocalypse on his pale horse, to potentially unleash pestilence on our floor. Living high up in an apartment tower, I smugly assured myself that we were safe. However, in our mid-seventies, we were in the most vulnerable pandemic group.

Then Amanda dropped her bombshell. 'I am moving back with my parents for two weeks because I want to put as much physical distance as possible between Bradley and me. Tomorrow he returns from Europe.'

With rising alarm in my voice, I enquired where his travels had taken him, hoping it might be Iceland, the Outer Hebrides or Lapland.

'Well, Bradley has been overseas for the last three weeks, having a lovely holiday with his parents in Italy, Spain and Britain,' she said without a hint of irony. 'Now the government is insisting that he self-isolate for two weeks. Although he's across the hall from you, he promises not to come out,' Amanda said, in an unsuccessful attempt to reassure me.

During the next two weeks, my greatest fear was that Bradley would develop cabin fever in the tiny one-bedroom apartment, go stir crazy and run screaming at me in our common hallway, before dashing to the elevator to escape. When Amanda left, Pam and I looked at each other in fear and said in unison, 'don't tell the kids.'

Nothing to Sneeze About

Kit Kelen

you wouldn't murder your old granny in her bed
or anyone else's for that matter

you wouldn't smother a baby with a pillow
in ordinary circumstances

take tissues from a terrible cough
or a bum that needs wiping

you wouldn't go into a crowded mall
and open fire indiscriminately with a semi-automatic weapon

you'd never turn off someone's life support system
(unless they'd specified when and under what circumstances
and you'd agreed reluctantly earlier on)

it is true sometimes you're hot
and you might take my breath away from time to time
you might give me fever now and then

but you wouldn't use germ warfare
just to win an argument

you wouldn't play Russian roulette for kicks
or make yourself a mummy in one of those dolls

you wouldn't start up your own zombie apocalypse
wouldn't want poxy zombie breath
you'd always clean your teeth

you wouldn't put children out on the street
take crumbs from their starving mouths

you wouldn't vote to end the economy
or curb the human species
(well, maybe you would)

if you wanted to top yourself
you'd think up something pleasanter

but anyway
I think you can see where this is going
you're not a complete evil shit are you?
so don't touch every bloody thing
and wash your hands after

stay the fuck home
don't catch COVID 19
do not pass it on!

Love Story

Shelley Stocken

Once I would notice
your hand on my back
the things on your bookshelf
your funny-shaped ears

Blushing with promise
I tripped on my feet
to get to the place where
the fairy tales go

Breathless, I traded
the catch in my throat
the gut-turning flutter
the thrill in my spine

Then to subsist on
your practical gifts
your boots in the hallway
your punctual snore

Tired from chasing
the heels of a dream
I asked if you wanted
a nice cup of tea

The Days

Gail Hennessy

On the first day planes stopped flying, birds began singing into the silence
ghosts inhabited the town

On the second day after the rain the rivers began flowing again,
etching the land with green valleys

On the third day in the fishing village doors were kept tightly closed;
boats knocked at the floating docks

On the fourth day grass grew through the cobblestones, up the walls of
the houses choked the chimneys with green velvet, snug as a warm blanket;
the windows in the houses stared blindly

On the fifth day the fishermen opened their doors, walked down to the
harbour, cast their nets from their boats, pulled them in over the side,
then hung them out to dry like cobwebs catching each dewdrop,
used their knives on the rocks and every oyster delivered a pearl

On the sixth day the children abandoned their devices and followed the
wind through the empty streets, danced into the mountains and played
in the clear pools at the foot of waterfalls, while back in the village their
parents waited for the sacred lotus to rise into sunlight

On the seventh day the children came home, the wind swept through
each open door the world began to breathe and the fishermen saw that it
was good for the earth had rested ...

Parcel

Greg Struck

When they told me of the minister's decision, they said I had an hour to get my things together. They said I could take one bag or parcel. I didn't have a bag—it had disintegrated after too many hard kilometres—so the decision was easy. They gave me some paper and string. Then it would be on to the bus—grey paint, barred windows—for the trip to what would be my new home. For how long?

Get my things together. My 'things'. The remnants of a life.

My passport. It once meant hope, possibilities. Travel. A new life elsewhere. Now it was just a testament to my place in a failed state, a place people thought of only when the nightly news brought the latest ghastly images of bombings and rubble.

Photos. My parents. Asif. And, of course, Yasmin. Faces from a time when cameras still caught smiles. When there were still things to smile and laugh about. The thought almost made me laugh.

A toothbrush and a comb. A shirt. Some underwear and a pair of socks. I remembered drawers full of shirts and underwear, demanding choices for my trips to the capital. Choices? When was the last time there had been a choice to make?

My copy of the Koran—a gift from my father. Once a foundation, a solid place in my life, a source of hope. Now, I wasn't so sure. There were too many unanswered questions.

A little money. A few dollars. Notes from a new country, bearing strange faces and unfamiliar creatures. But what would I buy?

And what was this? My old address book. Names from a different world. How many of them were still alive? Yusuf had drowned with fifty others when one of the first boats had tried to get through. Ali had been standing next to a bomber in a crowded market. Ismail was probably still at the bottom of the pile made when what had been the town's grandest building had been hit. And Yasmin. Yes … Yasmin. Better to let that thought go.

Then, my mother's apron. An odd thing to keep, but it was all I had of her, all I could find in what was left of the house. I looked at it again and could see her in the kitchen—the smoking fire, the endlessly boiling pots, the waft of cumin and rose water. I could still smell them.

That was it.

I tied the string as the guard opened the door and beckoned, his face impassive as always. I often wondered what sort of man lay behind that face. Sometimes I thought that I was only imagining that it was a man. Perhaps it was just an automaton who appeared from time to time to summon me to meals and hearings, punctuating the endless days with its arrival.

Outside, the bus waited.

The Red Blossoms

Rosemary Bunker

She breathed in the fear of the city, corralled on the balcony, green flashes of shrieking parakeets in the paper bark wall ignoring red blossoms, army of dandelions whirling and twirling batter her thyme, nothing to block COVID army, legions of red crab TV blossoms jostling on the floor, in the chair, her hair, aimed for her mouth, their entry, their survival in her lungs and her resistance a bar of soap like Don Quixote and she ninety years old in her V for vulnerable E for, she knew, expendable shirt no way out for her although she had listened, done what, more if she could in the supermarket, waiting at arm's length, feet marked in the queue, holding herself, stick woman paper sketch not brushing a surface, not touching a hand and how she missed that, the feel of skin, banned now, stroking and patting the cat, touch of life, checking the pet food, following the security guard single file down aisle three for toilet paper and the guard jokes if anyone coughs you'll shit yourselves from fear so the crowd cackled but this was no time, was it, for jokes and she clamped her mouth shut against red marauding crab blossoms and the heat, the sexual frenzy invisible in the supermarket, lurking on the empty shelves, the cash register as she waved her card, a magician no longer herself but a tree, absorbing and transforming night fog of fear that choked her dreaming of lovers, his hand on her thigh, of ham sandwiches and thick mustard that once was time for food and bottles of bubbly and red but not now, not on the edge, looking down, spades of rough-thrown earth marking the trench for her to fall when COVID hit, take no prisoners, she would go down but not to-day for the dentist accosted her outside the door with a thermometer proof of wellness required, pass friend, but the end would come soon enough, this certainty same as ever she did not want, feeling the thirst, the throat coated and closing, the lungs, hers no more resisting air, Canute a laugh, so she must stay here on the balcony, stay home, wash her hands, soap on blossoms like salt on slugs, coat herself with sanitiser and wait.

Stories and poems submitted to
Hunter Writers Centre Writing Contests

Tassel House Stairway

Lesley Harrison

We'd visit Grandpapa on Sundays at eleven thirty. Sharp. Religiously. As soon as Father shook Papa's hand and gave Mama a little bow under the sandstone arch of St Michael and St Gudula's cathedral, we'd set off clip-clopping the cobbles.

In precisely twelve minutes we'd pull up at the massive gothic portal. Waiting for Mama to disembark the carriage, I'd marvel at the door's black bolts until Uncle James's sun-washed smile emerged around the opening creaky timber: eyes first as always. The smell of roasting beef permeated the courtyard luring us to the third floor.

Skipping ahead of the others beyond the dip of the foot-worn marble step lay my favourite Sunday moment. My magical staircase to whereverland. Shadows and swirls that seasonally changed and followed me held my awed gaze. I'd stop and breathe in the smell of wax polish and soak in the chilly echo of the cavernous spiralling flight ahead. My Sunday best boots, sometimes feeling rather tight, tip-tapped up the stones in pursuit of the tweed, pocket watch and lemon-and-pipe-tobacco scent that was Grandpapa.

First to the top I'd burst into the reception room into his cheery seated embrace. Moments in time precious to us before the others arrived, he'd whisper, 'How's my little artist?' Each week was the same. Sherry for the grownups by the fire in winter and on the stoop in summer. A forever luncheon, then cards in the drawing room.

Well-trained to be out of sight and sound, I'd lose myself hypnotically in the rituals. Steam from the soup, ladled with precision by Martha, formed little disappearing spectres. The clang of the lifted cloche exposed more colour, texture and deliciousness than you could ever imagine for roast beef and vegetables. Puddings were Martha's specialty, with plump seasonal berries at their base and hot, smooth custard made with exotic vanilla from Madagascar oozing on the top. Occasionally a cloud-like sponge would nestle between the two.

Cards did not interest me. Staircases did so I'd sit at the top and imagine. I'd see architects who designed and drew them. I'd picture the quarry where the rocks became destined to be walked on, stonemasons who formed the steps, ironmongers who crafted the curls of lace and carpenters who whittled and sanded the wood to smooth perfection. My fingers traced the painted patterns down the walls as I'd tip-toe up and down as quietly as possible, afraid even to hum. One time, right at the top, a button pinged off my boots, tumbling, rolling and jumping all the way to the bottom in the perfect arc of the banister's curve. I watched everything with wonder. A little observer of life.

Those ritual, sensory Sundays steered me almost spiritually to a marvellous and blessed career as the first female architect in Brussels. For this enormous privilege I thank Sundays, Grandpa's whispering encouragement and the Tassel staircase.

Thank you speech.

Professor Mieke Van Groot.

Brussels University Awards 1930.

The Widow 1

Jan Dean

Forced to view some women, I might yawn and look away. This one is different. Although a curtsy is inapt, genuflect is warranted. Having drawn her many times, I am confident I have captured her essence, ready to transfer her image to the woodblock. In a lifetime, of the many positions a body configures, two predominate: first foetal, curled with back curved and bent limbs drawn up to the torso; and second, full length with legs extended in preparation for the grave. She is consecrated to suffering. War is relentless; it takes everything and leaves sorrow. I carve into the surface of a wooden slab, away from myself, using force to express fragility. Raised sections accept the rolled ink and pressure is applied, allowing ink to penetrate paper, acting like a stamp. My cuts stop short of her edge, blurring it a little. Flecks create both aura and depth, hinting the wood from which the composition was derived. The widow knew trauma. She felt pain like a cricket ball lodged in her stomach, directly beneath her heart. She wanted to lie on a bed in endless float, exiting time and earthly distraction. Her gnarled hands reflect drudgery. She is stark, her face already the mask of death. As if mummified, the widow's arms lie across her chest enfolding her son, a meaningful caress, yet he has vanished, forever gone.

Blaze and Stone

Kathryn Fry

Into the prison camp in Silesia, Messiaen
brought an angel cloaked in cloud; scored
rainbows into crystals, transposed harmony
into cascades of orange-blue calm. Mixed
though with dissonance, the most ungodly
vibrations to the ear, as if that angel had
run amok. From the cold and hunger, Olivier's
hair and teeth fell out, no wonder. Not though

his faith. With swollen fingers, he played
the dance of fury, a messiah with his chosen
three. They heard how he'd written in love,
saw how it gave them wings. All because
he'd listened to birdsong for hours
and wrote down every feathered note.

The Lost Sister

Magdalena Ball

Let's say there was a sister.
There is evidence to suggest it
though no one knows—no family get-togethers
no diary entries of tearful late-night gossip
letters on parchment paper written by candlelight
after her husband went to bed.

The journey was arduous
anything could have happened.

We know they were guilty of poverty, detained under
burden of persecution, searching for a new life.

All notes were written in invisible ink
in the solitude of the mind, the shadow self, lamplit.

The other self was tattered, unkempt, verklempt.

She might have covered the younger girl with her coat
saved her the best scraps, but still she disappeared.
There were so many diseases on the boat:
Cholera, the yellow cup-shaped crusts of Favus, Tuberculosis
or worse of all, Trachoma, which might get you sent back
blind, groping for a home that no longer existed
and every horror you ran from multiplied.

Avian Synthology

PJ Yeatman

The fireball dawn deslumberates
A flopsome bird of strilly bits
Immormous, pendle-limbed and godge
Kwaloka kwaw kwaw, it blaws

A skitting puff of wimmiwags
Confettified and interwhorled
Escapes capillarous treetops
And dipples into morning's glim

Along the wolden path there prinks
A fettle girl, galing glad songs
Which guile a shock of chitterdaws
That teem the maid like zippy juves.

The joyful dilly laughs with feen
Beflocked by plumerous wingdings
Not knowing where her ends begin
Or what is bird, or what is her

My Sister's Cloak

Ann Blackwell

Oh, dear God, this reminds me of my sister's Earth Cloak. I am appalled and she keeps sending me photos of it, which I try not to look at. An Earth Cloak is a chichi shroud. So, what does this mean for me? I am her 'identical' twin sister. We are both in our seventies.

The cloak is long, a gorgeous purple and green satin (feminist colours), and she is painting scenes from her life on it. Beautiful native birds, Australian flora and two elegant looking green and brown snakes slide down the front panels, their eyes staring at her feet. Yes, it is magnificent, but not for me.

Her eight-year-old granddaughter has done some wonderful paintings on it and thinks it's for a Halloween. She keeps asking if she can go trick-or-treating with Jen, wearing her magnificent cloak.

Now, I don't object to my sister making a cloak, that is not the issue. I am worried because I am her 'identical' twin and I mean identical, in every possible way. When she gets something medically wrong with her, I get it as well. We both take the same pills, for the same ailments. She looks like me, sounds like me, it is frightening. So why is she making this death cloak now? Is she saying something about the end of her life and therefore mine, or is it just a good time to make it? She is more comfortable talking about death, whereas I tend to skip through all the talk and pretend it is eons away.

She and her partner made an Earth Cloak for a friend of theirs who died aged forty-two years. This friend chooses to go all the way to Victoria to be buried. It is the only place where you can be buried standing up, apparently more environmentally sound. Her poor Italian mother was devastated as she wandered around a paddock amongst happily munching cows, trying to find her daughter. She had disappeared.

My granddaughter told me that you can be squashed into a cube, they plant you, and you become a tree.

'Gosh,' I said. 'That sounds terrific. But how do they squash you?'

She turned pale and ran out saying, 'I don't want to talk about it'.

I was wondering what would happen if I told my children I was making my own Earth Cloak? Their reactions would be very different.

My eldest daughter would freeze emotionally, intellectualise it, become efficient and talk about it, as though I was making it for someone else. She would be supportive, and instructive.

My son would start researching the whole subject, going back to Egyptian times and telling me about everyone who had ever had a shroud, and I would disappear into an amorphous mass of information, so he would not have to think about whom the cloak is for.

The youngest daughter would want to redesign it, argue about the politics of it, the color, the fabric, include all her children in painting, and we would have to throw a party to launch it, before I popped off.

So, guess what, I will avoid this conversation like the plague because I don't really care what I am be buried in.

About Nature

Chris Williams

The last remaining human
A poet, defiant in isolation
Watched Nature's inexorable descent
Shroud the village in wanton entropy.
Watched through one window intractable
The slow ivy crawl
Swallow buildings in monochrome green carpet.

At night, plastic tides lap and comfort him
The fish, they have abandoned him
Light, his only companion, returns as promised to blot away darkness
That lurks in grand palaces, little red books and ignorance.

The poet, now in a dusty cell, behind bars
For telling the truth
About Nature.

Imaging the Mind of Man Ray

D.M. Dorahy

Today I am taking photographs of my unique assemblage—a response to that inspiring phrase penned by Ducasse: '... the chance meeting on a dissecting-table of a sewing-machine and an umbrella.' A prototypical surrealist, he has juxtaposed the familiar to create an absurdity that incites us to ponder, or, maybe, to wonder.

I have gathered those few essentials that I need. A sewing machine: that efficiently engineered device which replicates the manual labour of hand-held threaded needle. The epitome of Modernity, it noisily speeds up the once painstaking process of sewing—to make or to mend—by rapidly replicating each little stitch, each a precise reproduction of the one before: trooping lines of uniformity.

This machine brings to mind memories of Papa, tailoring away in Brooklyn and asking me: '... what good is this art-making Emanuel, what is this bohemian life in Manhattan going to bring you, you gotta settle down, raise a family and earn a respectable living!'

I add an army blanket: relic of the trenches. I wrap the smooth, metallic device in the prickly-fibred fabric. Umbrella-like, the blanket is a canopy of calm.

Next a ball of twine. The string I unravel secures the blanket folds: looping, crossing over and under and around, twisting and turning. Intersections that mould and shape and sculpt the now hidden object which becomes an enigmatic icon, a covert homage to Ducasse, and perhaps, Papa.

Now the useless contraption is transformed, muffled: suffocated and silenced. No more rat-a-tat-tating, no more ghost-like reminders of machine guns firing. Impractical, irrational, a useless package this, something to be dismantled and discarded after the shooting of my film.

Then, only the photograph will remain. It may remind us that chance meetings of absurd realities occur constantly. Like the chance meeting on a battlefield of a bullet and a man.

The Blank Canvas

Dee Taylor

The cigarette brought scant relief. Margaret took a final drag then twisted the butt into the overflowing ashtray beside her cup of Irish Breakfast tea grown cold with the waiting. She stared into the green depth of her garden. Her mind as blank as the canvas in the room behind her strewn with tubes of paint, a collection of brushes and another overflowing ashtray. Lucy would be in later to clear the mess away and then attempt to sort the brushes into some order, even though she had told Lucy time and again to leave her stuff alone. She sighed at the plainness of it all. The bone crushing normality. Maybe it was time to give it away and enjoy the quiet ebbing of her life. No surprises left, just a slow decline into the expectations of her age and all that accompanied it.

She heard a quiet rustle in the garden next door. Ben picking some innocent plant to sacrifice into the latest salad fad, she supposed. Her knees were stiff this morning. She gave them a brief rub and shifted her position in the wicker chair with the peeling cream paint and studied the toes of her worn slippers. She liked their scruffiness, not thrown away because they were old. Life.

The adjoining garden gate creaked. No, she thought, she could not handle his positive platitudes. Not today. She hauled herself upright and hobbled inside, leaving the cup and ashtray for Lucy.

The quietness of the house held her in a familiar embrace. The slight mustiness reminded her of old clothes and of the secret hidey holes in her grandparent's house in her favourite hide-and-seek games with her brother. They're all gone now.

She stared at the virgin canvas. Nothing. She shuffled the paint brushes and thrust them down into the white and blue china mug with the Chinese design. Back to the canvas. Still nothing.

Perhaps another cup of tea. As the water rose in crescendo she arranged the apples in the fruit bowl, looking for inspiration. No, that won't work, she mused.

A loud knock at the front door. Margaret glanced up at the large timber framed clock. Lucy has a key and she wasn't due for another half hour, best to ignore it.

Back to that damned canvas. She stared at its inhospitable surface and pursed her lips. What could she do with it? Throwing it against the wall seemed a possible solution. She lit a cigarette.

The minutes ticked on. A key turned in the lock.

'Hello Margaret, how are we today?'

We? I wasn't aware there were two of me, thought Margaret. 'Hmmph. I've had better mornings.'

'What's wrong?'

'Oh, don't mind me Lucy, I'm in a mood this morning.'

'Well this might cheer you up, look what Ben from next door left for you at the front door.'

She turned to see Lucy holding a large basket of pomegranates. Margaret smiled.

Looking Back

Diana Pearce

My memories are filled with images
that flicker
like fractured light past
photos of unremembered instances,
past my personal realities.

My brother and I hold hands
stare unsmiling at the camera,
I am four, tossing grain to feed the hens,
I straddle a large horse, my uncle has the reins;
familiar faces, the rest forgotten

I recall
watching my grandmother
plucking feathers from a beheaded hen,
riding my pony to help my father muster sheep,
bottle-feeding orphan lambs and poddy calves.

I piece together the fragments
that dance through my mind,
remake into a whole
patterned by choice.

Skeleton Leaf

Magdalena Ball

Age came with no preamble
the thinning of tissues, intricately laced veins
where skin was once smooth.

It was still possible to see the girl in her bone structure
looking outward, sienna ferrotype, always the eyes
bigger than you'd expect in such a small face
full with something recognisable, unsayable, longing
and resignation, carried together, held in tension.

Already the body was shrinking, the world blurring
she needed help up the steps, stumbled against the door
burned her arm rendering schmaltz.

Sat and sat and wouldn't stand for fear of falling.
She leaned against the arm of the big chair
feeling the lightness of her imprint.

From that spot she could conjure
a lifetime, any moment she thought lost
ghostly against the window
the spaces and places she'd known and left
sheer, timeless, at the end of a finger
frail but no less real, no less solid.

Inhospitable Landscape

Ellen Shelley

Today you scan the pavement
        like a body waiting to be told
what is and isn't working.
        On the phone I hear your chords running
low on fuel. A voice-box almost gone.
        Lines of *I am dying.* Questions
that raise hairs on the back of my neck.
        When you visit, would you like to go
through my wardrobe? Years ago, I would have jumped at the chance
        but you would not have had reason
then, for someone to take the clothes off your back, that now no longer fit
        unresponsive tumours, the wrong type of hormones,
a life shined out of reserves. I park outside your house
        like a thief and count my guilty blessings.
Weeds are pushing up through cement like labour,
        unstoppable—

Many Hunter Writers Centre members have focused on publishing books over the last few years. Here is a selection:

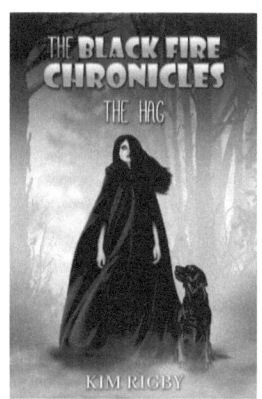

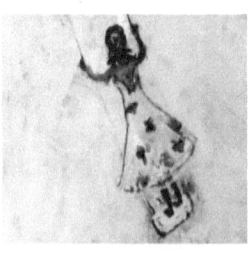

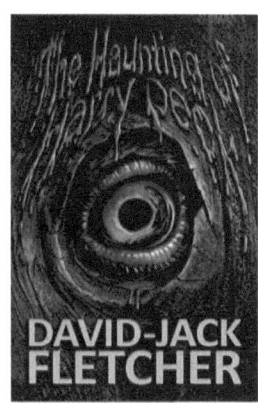

The Adventures
of the
Louth Park Mob

20 short stories about growing up around Maitland.
N.S.W. in the 1960's and 1970's.

written by ...
Nick Fairleigh
and
Paul Doherty

Editing, layout and images by David S Soffer

Cherry Chicken
Chocolate Kitchen
Poems on Play

Rebecca Trowbridge
illustrated by Caitlin Bales

SHOOTING
THROUGH
Campo 106 escaped POWs
after the Italian armistice

Katrina Kittel

PIXIE DUST
a memoir
Bronwyn MacRitchie

Matron Ida Greaves
'a right daughter of Australia'

By Clarisse M Bramley

HEALING
OURSELVES AND
OUR EARTH
THE REAL HEALTH INSURANCE AND THE
DIARY OF A NATURAL THERAPIST

PAULA MORROW

Judy Johnson
Dark Convicts

AVERIL DRUMMOND

SLOAM

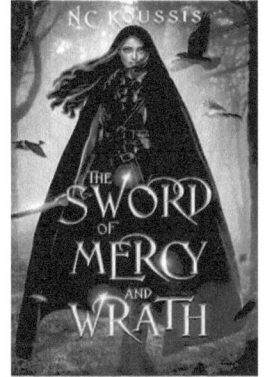

NC KOUSSIS

THE
SWORD
OF
MERCY
AND
WRATH

Albert

Ann Blackwell

I am eighteen, this is my first job and I want to make a good impression. I have been here four weeks. The city of Johannesburg is buzzing outside, and I am feeling very grownup. I watch the three white male staff chat and laugh at the front counter. My job is to give them spare parts information, which I have in a cabinet on cards in front of me.

Answering the phone, I notice Albert standing in front of me. He is a tall, good-looking African man, with trendy dreadlocks and a gentle smile. Albert does all the heavy lifting and carrying of spare parts for the three white males on the front counter.

'Madam can you give me the number of this engine part please.'

I point that I'm on the phone when the other phone starts ringing. I feel flustered with two phones wanting information and now Albert's waiting for me as well. I whisper to Albert 'answer the other phone' and ask them to wait. He shakes his dreadlocks with a definite no.

'Please Albert,' I urge.

He picks up the black Bakelite phone and starts to speak, when the two men from the front counter, rush over and one hits him with a crashing blow across the head. Albert falls to the floor and the other man kicks him in the ribs. He does not move.

'You black bastard, how dare you,' fumes the white clerk.

I am frozen in fright. My heart is thumping, my anger boiling, I can't speak. The white males are glaring at me. Everyone in the office has come out and are staring at me.

'This is a "white" phone and blacks are not allowed to touch it. Albert should know that,' the clerk says, red in the face.

'But it is my fault, I asked him to answer the call.'

'So, you want his filthy black mouth on your white phone, do you?' he says, exploding with rage.

'There is nothing wrong with Albert's mouth, you dickhead. How dare you hit him for no reason. Are you mad?'

He looks at me with absolute horror and says,

'Oh shit, are you some sort of kaffir lover? I should have killed the bastard.'

The whole office is now staring at me with disgust. I feel helpless and embarrassed. A woman is rubbing the phone viciously to get Albert's mouth off it. I have never been part of this savage cruelty before. I see racism every day, but it has been more verbal than physically violent. They drag Albert behind the shelves and leave him under a blanket.

Albert is tightly bound up by Apartheid Laws, and he is not seen as human by these people. Under that blanket there is simmering silence and burning hostility.

The next day I see Albert and whisper, 'I'm so sorry.' He walks past me, his head held high, but does not utter a word. I realise that I am part of his problem. I must leave this horror; leave a country I love and leave Albert to sort it out. Nelson Mandela is still in gaol for another twenty-eight years.

Autumn Ghost 1

Nicole Rain Sellers

You wink and dissolve in sepia
mulch underfoot, a velvet
of bark and twigs, ash and fog.
Spring will weave something dewy
from the vacated spiderweb life
you cast across my path, will wrap
the house in ivy, gleam snail trails,
swell snow peas, drip into my coffee,

push me to the beach to find in sand
your skeleton, some permanent imprint
of whole leaf, snowflake or spiderweb.
You harvested heirloom seeds, grafted
your gametes onto my spine, your shape
refracted and scattered in droplets
wherever I swim, patterned in liquid nets
or frozen steam, according to season.

My moth-eaten, backward heart dives
for the rules you made, unearths a family
tree mirrored in seaweed and leaf litter,
blood and bone, roots wider than its branches.

Sand

Diana Pearce

In the cold time
neither sleeping nor waking
I hold the sands of our words
mould them shape them
but they slip through my fingers
shift on the wind
to other dunes.

In the darkness
I will write them
on your eyelids
and you will read them
as you sleep.

Bunbury Summer

Julia Brougham

We were back living in Whadjuk Noogar country again. It was Birak, season of First Summer. Christmas Day had just gone and it was school holidays. Cousins had come from their farm for a one week stay after the wheat harvest. Beach time!

Our road fizzled out at the base of a high sand dune and became a track up past a black and white peppermint stick lighthouse, down through rocks and stretches of beach spinifex grass with spiky-ball flower heads. Around the curve of another dune and there was the wide sweep of Mabakoort, the Indian Ocean. Deep blue, so blue it looked like you could pull up a bucket of it and paint with it. We'd crossed it by ship two months before.

Our favourite beach was sheltered by long curving arms of rock that slowed the waves to a gentler swish. Throw down the towels and race each other into the water.

You'd get over the sun-hot sand that slowed you down, burning your feet so you hopped from one to another to lessen the pain, into the lemon-green shallows specked with bits of seaweed. Now the wave-laid ripples underfoot smoothed out and you felt each piece of broken shell and fragment of old worn coral littered there.

You would flinch at the first cold shock of the waves that splashed your chest as you pushed towards the place where water and sun-bleached sky dissolved into each other and the salty iodine tang was filling your nose. This was the right time to let your knees buckle, let mother ocean slide up over your shoulders, go back to the place you were before you were born out of your own tiny ocean, carrying it with you as the water you are mostly made of.

Splash and dive and muck about, testing that our toes could still touch bottom. When we needed heat and our fingers were white and wrinkled we'd go back to the sand to towel ourselves warm before poking around the rock crevices looking for small crabs to annoy. In the rock pools we'd look down into the glass-clear water at red and green seaweeds, shells and trapped fishlings. If there were sea anemones, we would dare each other to put a finger into an open one to feel it clasp and cling with its slow waving tentacles.

Once we found a piece of green glass that had been chipped and rounded by the ocean into a Rodin-esque sculpture the size of my thumb. It sits on my shelf now, a memento of transition between two continents divided by that deep, deep blue ocean.

My Friend Masie

Ann Blackwell

I lay on my stomach in the long grass hiding from my grandmother. I was hot all over. I could hear her tell Lena, her servant, to find me. My eleven-year-old heart beat against the damp earth, but I knew she would not find me. Lena stepped over me and walked on down the hill saying, 'She is going to kill you when she finds you.'

I had picked at the wallpaper above my bed, until the pink March lily had become a black hole. I wanted to be sent back home for the rest of my school holidays, but 'the witch' had already told me, 'Your mother does not want you at home.' The sadistic satisfaction on her face drove me to pick at the lily above my bed.

Through the long grass I saw my African friend Masie walking down the hill with a little pot on her head. She was two years older than me but she was my best friend. I raced down the hill and asked if she could come and play. Masie lived in a mud hut at the bottom of my grandparents' property and her mother and father worked for them. 'I don't want you playing with those filthy black children.' My grandmother had groaned at me. 'They are disgusting.'

Masie and I, our arms around each other, walked into the rainforest, where it was cool and damp. Giant green trees huddled together, hiding us from the hot sun and prying eyes.

Bright streams ran between the rocks, crystal clear, cold water lapping our feet. We were surrounded by the smell of moss and forest wildflowers.

I started hitting the stream angrily with a stick and said, 'I don't like my grandfather.'

'Why?'

'He touched me inside my knickers,' I mumbled, hot with embarrassment.

'Oh, what did you do?' Masie's eyes as big as saucers.

'I jumped off his medical couch and kicked him really hard on his skinny shins, then ran away.'

Masie looked at me then laughed. She slid off the rock giggling and I was furious.

'Why are you laughing Masie? I don't know much about these sorts of things, but that's very wrong, isn't it?' I said angrily.

Masie stood there and looked at me and I suddenly felt a distance push its way between us. I was puzzled and said crossly,

'Masie, what's wrong? Why are you being so silly about this?'

Masie turned around slowly, then sneered at me. 'He's been doing that to me since I was ten years old.'

I felt my insides contort with fear and anger.

'But why didn't you tell me. I could have …'

'Because I am black,' Masie cried. 'No one would believe me.'

She turned around and walked off carrying her berries on her head, leaving me standing there furious and hurting. I knew then that I had lost my best friend, as I watched her walk home down the hill. I went in the opposite direction.

Jigsaw Memory

Cedar Whelan

Carrying a bag of jumbled jigsaw pieces.
No idea what
the big picture
should look like.

Knowing pieces are missing—
some to be found,
many lost forever.
The impact of traumas.

Often what I do recall and share,
others contradict.
I simply have to concede.
They're more likely correct.
After all,
I'm the mad one.

So hard to accept
there's a lot
I'll never know.

Let it go, they say.

Maybe one day
it will let go of me.

The Wonderful Taste of Non-Water

Julie Simpson

Aaah-h-h! The glassy flow of fresh water trickling down
your throat a sudden slurp of saturated air a liquid strip
of wet cling film backlit transparent silver streaming
falling from clouds to join the lake/river/creeks/dams
imperceptible ripples of coolth ready to replenish my
breathless body cells & recharging other invisibles:
my sweet soul / life force longings / my thirsting
for this wonderful non-taste of cool clear water.
Consider the acrobatics when swallowing great
gulps of wetness in jerky responses glug-glug
or snaking down throats in uncoiling pleasure
s-w-a-l-l-o-w or bringing the luxury of much-
needed sip sip sips of icy re—fresh—ment.
Deep drinking delight that gives the feeling
of ultimate lightness with its sweet bouquet
of nothing at all turning gasping breaths
into song between our simple ah-ha-hahs
of relief / / / / / whenever it starts to rain.
/ / / /
/ / /

Memory

Rosemary Bunker

I am an old woman. I drift through the rooms in my house and feed on memories that always live there. They are my life now. I caress the red and golden beads of an amber necklace, still fired by the Silk Road sun at Tashkent. The stench of the animal market there has long since gone. My feet sink into the coarse grey wool of the rug woven by nomad women in Iran. The tree of life design has faded but I see an illuminated green pomegranate tree, heavy with fruit. No ugly memories live in my memory kingdom. They have been bedded, have become the compost from which I have grown.

Memories of childhood sweeten my life. Bleak scenes of rows and violence at home and school, the cane and the trap, have melted into background noise. I see myself as a confident child who knew her place in the world. God ruled, Mr. Menzies was in charge and father, his henchman. We lived in the country, an ideal place where a cow with liquid brown eyes gambolled on the common where we played. Roosters crowed and fresh veggies kept growing on the dinner plate. Never mind the drought, the grasshoppers and the cost of petrol.

I played all day on the common, in the creek or on the back verandah overlooking the world. A pudgy four-year old with dark plaits, I see my friend, Dora, playing with a stranger—how dare she!—on the common. A club with many heads—treachery, jealousy, exclusion—hammered me. Scarlet flames of anger set fire to our woodheap as every fragment of my observer's body coalesced into one tight shape that screamed vengeance.

Rage blinded me as I stumbled to my work table but my mind was clear. I grabbed a black crayon and tore a ragged bit of paper from my drawing pad. The tussle with words was brief. I did not know 'bitch' but wild animals were odious and hateful for my purpose.

DORA IS A LOIN

DORA IS A TIGGER

DORA WENT FOR A WALK

AND SHE DID NOT TAKE ME

The words, the mastery of the medium, thrilled me. I raced inside to show mum. As she read it aloud to her morning tea friends, I cringed and twisted to avoid invisible arrows that stung. She read 'loin' and 'tigger' in a funny voice. She was laughing and I was hurting. How could she? My heart beat a wild rhythm as my stiff lips smiled.

I crawled to my bedroom and despaired at the wall that separated me from my mother. Ninety years later, misplaced trust and ambiguity still cloud that relationship but, like her, I am a mother. I gloss the judgement and see her as the best mother she could be.

But sometimes, when I feel again the passion of that four-year old, I wonder what happened to her fledgling career as a writer.

Low Chroma

Magdalena Ball

Eyelids down, body on damp rock.
There is no day or night, only rotation.
This close, ultraviolet might be visible
only to a hummingbird, fired in a harlequin kiln
against hillside moss, in the gap
between desire and memory, a homage to absence.

From here there is no longing, only breath
steady against filtered light, where forest is body,
an undifferentiated block, line and form, carbon dioxide and oxygen.

Outside this space, there is so much noise it is impossible
to pick out shards of meaning, to emerge unscathed
from the undergrowth, to re-engage with the river.

Sound has gravity, travelling through solid rock as wind
thunder, argument, breaking through the silence, punching in.
If humans could photosynthesise, taking nutrients from the sun
would we change, become greener, not just our skin, voices softening
to a whisper, linking roots beneath the surface, healing.

Encounter

Ronald Atilano

I remember the slow procession of boats and their black nets
That evening at the old pier, when, having fallen asleep
On a bench, I suddenly woke up from a strange dream,
Faintly recalling an encounter with a man at that same spot,
A man who looked like me, and who, after an argument,
Drew a revolver and shot me to death, then dragged my body
Into the water. As I sank, he calmly sat down on the same iron bench,
Gazing at the passing boats. The sun had set, the wind sighing.
The pained joy that it had all just been a dream, the stars
A scattered chorus above me. I walked back home.
For a number of days, I didn't leave my room,
Avoiding the company of friends. I grew weary
Of my old causes, wary of any gestures of generosity,
Stopped smoking, religiously saw the doctor for the smallest cough
Or irregular heartbeat. In time, my voice grew coarse,
As if a crow had been trapped, thrashing wildly, in my lungs.
These days, when I look in the mirror, I recognise
The man from that night, the criminal I have become,
As my old self lies submerged under the drifting boats,
From time to time getting tangled in their mournful nets.

Pet Hate

Brenda Proudfoot

Marcia ambushes me, the moment that I turn into our driveway. 'It's a tragedy,' she says. 'Winston was taken before his time.'

Her lip quivers and I feel an unfamiliar pang of sympathy for her—until she reaches into my car window and shoves my shirt label down the back of my neck. I bristle. The woman is insufferable. A retired teacher who still thinks she's on playground duty.

Marcia and I are neighbours. We moved into 17A and 17B Ironbark Avenue more than five years ago, but she still refuses to call me Sue.

You know the kind of place I mean—two duplexes crammed onto a tiny suburban lot with a narrow row of agapanthus lining the edge of the driveway. Hardly the ideal place for an incontinent bulldog to live. Winston's favourite place to relieve himself was on my recycling bin.

I lost my ragdoll cat a couple of weeks after we moved in. I'd just put Bella down on a patch of grass near my clothesline when that wretched dog belted after her. She disappeared over the Colorbond fence, never to be seen again.

'Good riddance!' Marcia said when I told her Bella was unlikely to survive in the wild.

Well, now it's her turn to suffer. Marcia dabs at her eyes with a tissue. 'The trouble is, Susan, there's nowhere to bury him here.'

She's given me a delicious idea. I adopt a suitably mournful expression and sweet-talk Marcia into agreeing to having Winston preserved for posterity. I tell her one of my school friends is a taxidermist who has won prestigious awards for her artistry.

Her eyes light up before she twigs that this might be an expensive option.

'I'll see what I can do. Margaret is one of my closest friends—she'll probably do it for mate's rates.'

Marcia purses her lips. I can see her cogs going round. As if I'd have friends.

'This way,' I continue, 'Winston will always be here with you. I know he'll be different, but it might be a comfort to you, all the same.'

She agrees to think about it, and I go inside and give Molly a ring. She was a terror at school, and I'm confident that she'll be only too happy to help me execute my plan. Our teachers used to call her Margaret, but she's always preferred Molly.

In the end Marcia agrees and I take Winston's remains to Molly's place and we talk over some options for poses.

I'm still chuckling as I get back into my car. Molly hasn't changed. Her suggestions are more wicked than mine.

Marcia is so excited about having Winston reincarnated that she can't wait for the day when he'll arrive.

When I hear the delivery van pull into our shared driveway, I savour the scene. Marcia takes the carton inside and lifts her bulldog out of the protective packaging. Winston's glass eyes bulge as he strains to lick his privates.

The Hang-Out

Therese Lloyd

We would converge in the afternoon, uniformed dresses hiked up much higher than allowed between nine and three. Our tanned and shaven legs hoping to attract attention—who's we did not know. Retouches of mascara and eyeliner had been made on our sojourn from school, darker than our light application in the morning. Hair bounced, happy to be freed from its regulatory band. Together we would throw in coins stealthily scrounged from benches at home. There was a table out front. If an unsuspecting had perched themselves there before our descent, we would hover like gulls waiting for a crumb. They left, of course, overwhelmed by our loudness and body spray that swam through the air in its fruity frenzy. Davo would be behind the counter as we swanned in and placed our usual order. His large stomach, hanging over his pants would roll, slowly ebbing up and down as he jiggled our chips and wiped sweat away with his chubby hand. He was always friendly, in a funny fatherly way. Shaking his head at our giggles and sighs.

As I drive through the street to visit mum, I pass Davo's. The name, once emblazoned in red, is faded, only visible to those who would look. A new banner hangs below—'Café 95'—with an invitation for coffee and cake. I glimpse polished benches carrying glass cabinets filled with delectable delights. People lounging in modern chairs. I can hear our talk, our chatter. Life's plans—when we would get out. Some did, some did not. Three are gone now. Two lost too soon, before they could dance. Another we farewelled, had to leave her babes behind. And the rest of us are scattered through distance and time, each walking our own path away from the past.

Two Tritina

Mark Liston

(For Walter and Mabel Smith)

1. Rain Clocks Time

A dripping ceiling is counting rain,
in the hollow hallway it is clocks.
But both remind you of time.

You can't try sleeping away the time.
This week in bed you listen to rain
in bed it is the endless clock.

Watching the ceiling stain, the clock
Reminds, you are missing Mabel all the time.
You lose count counting drips of rain.

But you will sleep soon: rain clocks time.

2. (The) Sun Shines Now

I wake with the light of the sun
and sense your smile as it shines.
You tell me it is all fine now.
And I can open my heart again now
and feel the warmth of your sun.
Oh, how this bedroom we love, shines.

You return with the light, it shines
in your hair, in your eyes and my soul now.
I am whole again; you have brought the sun.

We are whole again, now the sun shines.

Failed to Provide

Ellen Shelley

They searched for you on my belly

your last watery breath
a breach in the womb
extinguishing your light

I rolled over suffering against the blank hospital wall

condolences arrived in
blue   lavender   white
mingling on the kitchen bench

stemmed soldiers
scented guilt
pity immersed in glass jars

grief sparks such clarity
the spoken and unspoken

your memories would fill a solitary page
a button up pinny   vapour footprints

you were just passing by

in time
web like fascia bind
around striated muscles
absolving our pain

we gathered around you with
prayers   poetry   silence

a shroud of earth
a tiny boxed frame
a nameless man   shovelling you a home
I had failed to provide.

Walking Through Time

Julia Brougham

The Old Man walks in

Spring shadow and light

Heel toe footsteps and swinging arms mark

Time's measured flow,

Sequencing his yesterdays, todays,

and uncertain destiny.

Yet entropy of passing days,

from urgent, untried, loose-limbed youth

to three score years and ten

is memory

unconfined,

unconstrained,

by arbitrary intervals of arrowed Time.

He slips those bonds at will,

and walks,

unbounded,

through all his Springs.

Promise on a Wet and Lonely Night

Justine Bird

The streets were empty. Shops shut. Even the fish and chip shop had closed its doors for the night.

You couldn't miss it was a fish and chip shop. It said so emphatically on the window, three times in different colours, fonts and sizes, including once in neon lights. Another sign under the awning, outside the shop, 'Fish & Chips Hamburgers Grilled Fish.' If fish or hamburgers didn't do it for you, they also ran to fried chicken. I preferred the fish and chips with a Greek salad, even tabbouleh if on offer. I could taste it now, pity the shop was closed.

The shop wasn't large. It had a long counter down one side and behind it the vats for deep frying, hot plates for grilling fish or hamburgers, and a rotisserie for chicken. Not sure a rotisserie *fried* chicken exactly, guess that was poetic licence. Along the other wall, next to the drinks cabinet ran a long bench with a few stools so you could eat there if you wanted or just sit and wait for your order, making idle talk. On the walls were menus, pricelists and images of Greece, brilliant white and blue.

For convenience you could phone in your order and collect when ready. It seemed a good idea if you were an organised sort of person. But to me the fish and chip shop was a neighbourhood hub that you wanted to visit, regularly, with an excuse to linger and see who was about and what was going on.

It was always interesting to read the cards, mostly handwritten, placed in the shop front window. Work wanted, odd jobs, babysitting, dog walking, second-hand cars, bicycles and baby things for sale. Some cards hadn't changed in a while, blue ink faded with sunlight. There were a few new cards since last week. The hourly rate for gardening had gone up— inflation I guess. Could I afford a couple of hours' help in the garden? Maybe I'll take the number down for future reference.

On wet nights like tonight the shop looked forlorn. No one about, only distant headlights of cars that turned the corner before heading this way, the muffled sound of tyres shooshing through water-logged gutters.

Among the new cards in the shop window I read, "Business for sale. Great location, long lease, reasonable rent. Reliable turnover. For details, contact proprietor within." What would I do with this business? Jazz it up a bit? Repaint, improve lighting? Add some outdoor dining, sun umbrellas for those long hot summer days. Plants for shade and wellbeing. Perhaps some music—quiet jazz or classical—to be a little different, distinctive, fun to visit. A few tweaks to the menu—add some desserts, gelati or Baklava perhaps, my favourite.

Could a fish and chip shop change my life? Promise comes in all shapes and sizes, even fish and chip shops on a wet and lonely night.

Two Birds, One Nest
Katrina Kittel

She blurted out tumbled-up names and nouns, my war-bride mother, battling her stroke-stumped speech. She kept tissue box tops, shopping dockets and mint-lolly wrappers to tell me her shopping list. She hid unpaid bills in the pantry to fade and flatten under the '50s-green lino shelves, waiting for me.

She patted paw-paw cream on her lower legs—gashed and gulfed by ulcers—willing them to heal. Her beige bandages peeked through the side-slits of her maxi-length flower-print kaftan. She didn't flap about the surgery to sever and stump-stitch her legs. When she woke, morphine-drenched, she lifted her stumps like puffy fingerless hands waving a piss-off to pain. She learnt to slip on prosthetic legs, my gutsy mother, to stand steady with two sticks and walk straight.

She'd steer her wheelchair through our kitchen then stretch up and over and into the kitchen sink, cleaning my dishes. She'd secretly wash some of her laundry, when it worried her, sometimes popping it into the oven to dry. She'd plonk three teaspoons of sugar into her cup, pour apple juice onto her cereal, and sip pharmacy-bought codeine cough syrup like it was lolly water.

She drove her chair into our home elevator and head off to bingo. When a taxi driver rushed and slammed her wheelchair into the kerbside, propelling her to the ground, slamming her buttocks from wheelchair to concrete, she sat silent like a wave-slapped seagull too stunned to flap. I stood silent, my hands clawing our veranda handrail, willing the driver to squat down and lift her.

She could easily slide from wheelchair to her shower-chair, until her rotator cuffs run out of puff. Her occupational therapist was right: she must leave the house for rehabilitation; she may not come back. I could not look into her brown, deep eyes. She wouldn't want to leave. Her eyes wanted to stay sharply focused on me—the new-mother—and the new baby. She doted, loved, doted. Two strong women in one nest, a psychologist declared, when I sobbed about my creeping estrangement from my mother, and of my dangerous selfish thoughts. I felt suffocated and tired, a new mother making difficult desperate decisions for her mother. My tired, old-hand mother was too speech-stumped to flap. She drove her chair into our home elevator, thinking she'd be fixed and coming home soon. Our mother roles flipped. I floundered.

She stooped into death's sleep with a shudder, my tenacious mother, in her late-night hospital room. I sighed and it did not feel right. I lifted a soggy tissue, like a wartime-mother farewelling her child-soldier. One of my brothers came, her youngest son, but he was far too late. For ten years my mother's secret things slept in her chest of drawers, in our home, waiting for me.

Strangeness

Jan Dean

See that pile of jigsaw pieces over there? That's me.
You'll patiently sort through over a great length of
time and find more than one puzzle with crucial pieces
missing. It seemed to happen suddenly, but I know deep
down it took a few years. You know what I mean. I'm
talking about the pandemic; war and rumours of war;
unseasonal weather of great impact that saw glaciers
melt in the Northern Hemisphere causing oceans to
rise. Horrific temperatures and drought in the Southern
Hemisphere came to a fearsome halt with deluges of
biblical proportions, bringing repeated floods. Advanced
age exacerbates matters. Who wouldn't be anxious when
nothing makes sense? Isolation made me madder than
before. Who wouldn't discard a few pieces of a distressed
and rebellious self, sweeping them under the floormats?
There's no denying the nagging feeling no one can put me
back together again.

Stories and poems written for exhibitions at
Lighthouse Arts

dear whales

Nicole Rain Sellers

if humans ever divert you
or sonar dupes you to beach
we request that you continue
your migration by sky detour
over our harbour & gardens
across the evening dunes

    float above newcastle city
    spin slowly in pink twilight
    swim like blimps over traffic
    our upturned faces awestruck
    angle your baleens downward
    stare us straight in the eyes

        we will attempt to trick you
        pester your ridges with kites
        blow signals out of chimneys
        lure you into coastal baths
        wave & shout on scaffolds
        dangle hooks from cranes

    please pay us little attention
    wield your barnacled flippers
    threaten slaps of your flukes
    sing into our fragile eardrums
    shatter our windows & bricks
    let nothing stand in your way

take a shortcut to antarctica
reach cleaner currents & feast
compose new melodious codas
birth robust calves & remember
we treat you as well as we can
despite having smaller brains

First Encounter

Diana Pearce

From cliff tops and lighthouses, beachfront homes
and purpose-built boats
we watch them pass.

In my youth they existed in Jonah's journey
Ishmael's words, illustrations of whaling in Twofold Bay,

As adults we drove north, to Hervey Bay,
joined others on a special boat   sailed into the bay   waited,

a great humpback appeared   swam to our boat,
lingered alongside   then dived   disappeared
a moment of disappointment
then   gasps of relief as it emerged the other side
great head and great eye watching   waiting.

So   it continued   like a game
up and under   to and fro   its eye always watching
boat rocking as we swarmed across the decks
to see   to be close   to wonder.

Until   there was no return   its 'game' over
only faint ripples where it left us,
elated   our spirits uplifted
deepened by this sublime encounter.

BLUE

Karen Whitelaw

Bluebottles sting. My brother stamps on them when they're marooned along the tide line, and cheers when they pop. He swims amongst them like a male Atë and when they seek revenge he just peels off their clinging blue tentacles and dives back in.

Likely you'll find me on those bluebottle days collecting shells. Or sitting on dry sand burning. Or turning blue in the cold nor'easter waiting for him. I pick off his poisonous barbs as he dares me in. *You're dead a long time!*

Until he took off backpacking around Asia last year, we were always together. I stayed, joining a firm in the main street as an insurance underwriter. His Instagram 'thing' was taking selfies on crumbling cliff tops. I calculated the risks and deleted the app.

Even during our birth he careered down the tunnel too soon, impatient, eager, first, and I, terrified, had to be wrestled out with steel. If you asked my brother, he'd say I'm the one who always gets stung.

Sunday Blues

Brenda Proudfoot

A pair of blue-faced honey eaters in a gum tree slide their beaks under strips of peeling bark. Their olive-green backs merge into the foliage unlike the iridescent blue streaks around their eyes.

A juvenile honey eater plunges off the fence and lands on a red grevillea. He hangs upside-down to drink the nectar. His face is still olive-green, a colour my mother detested.

I was nine when Mum discovered she was having a 'change of life' baby. Aunty Glenys gave her a dragon green maternity smock and some unsolicited advice. She knew someone who would take care of Mum's little problem.

My twelve-year-old brother hated that smock with a passion.

'Mum—you can't wear that! It's the colour of baby poo.'

In recent years, Mum loved sitting on our front veranda where she could see the blue of the water through the trees. The sparrows, thrushes and blackbirds in Auckland were a dowdy bunch, whereas a parade of colourful characters sashayed through our lakeside garden: galahs, rainbow lorikeets, eastern rosellas and sulphur-crested cockatoos.

It's Sunday afternoon: a drizzly, grizzly day after a summer of relentless heat. I want to tell Mum about the blue-faced honey eaters, to tear strips off Glenys and remember my late brother's wit. I'm dying to pick up the phone and have a chinwag with my mother. But she's no longer there to answer my call.

Whale Hymn

Judy Johnson

Praise, as pulsing wet
we stretch the rubbered light

over our triton backs.
And at dusk, give in to the hectic rush

of mucous and air in our blowholes,
geysering the salmon shoals in the sky.

Praise the sudden upturned snout derailing
a slippery thirty-ton train at a leap.

Praise the outlines of our bodies
as we breach, eclipsing the sun,

limned with gold and barnacles,
like eremitic gods emerging

from a dark sabbatical
amongst the crusty oysters.

Praise the first word which was suffused
with the mollusc-and-brine

ker*thump* of emotion
and not the dry arithmetic of meaning.

Praise the gentle, hissing lace of repetition,
the ocean's breathing in and out

and the slow water-test of our engines
at rest and swim, the internal rap

of enormous knuckles, corrugation by corrugation,
down the galvanised tanks of our hearts.

Nothing more to know of joy than its leap.
Nothing more of sorrow than a blue surface

left undisturbed, and over it, the commonplace
fish market shriek of gulls.

Blue Like

Linda Harding

Blue like a blue moon, rare lunar blue.

Blue like the place where the sky meets the sea, that place that disappears as you arrive. Near and distant blue

Blue like my sapphire engagement ring, scratched from years of wear, still solid. Old love blue.

Blue like the velvet jackets in our wedding photos, with matching blue bow ties: all so cool. Fad blue, rad blue.

Blue like a child's mouth after a blue lolly, opened wide, shown with joy. 'See my blue mouth, mum!' Childhood blue.

Blue like the pacific waters of a beach on an ordinary day. Deceptively ordinary blue.

Blue like his bright blue eyes, entering the blue sea, closing forever, forever. A vanishing blue

Blue like Mary's blue veil in the icons, suffering mother to a suffering God. Bereft blue. I've worn that blue.

Blue like sadness in a colour, like the delicate wing of a dragonfly, hovering always hovering. That blue.

Whale Fall

Julie Simpson

'A Whale!   Down it goes & more and more …
up goes its tail!' the haiku poet *Buson* cried
as an ancient leviathan left the light.
One final blow a backward roll as a Titanic black shadow
larger than a shipwreck reverses spiralling through each
darkling zone …… A slow-twister dropping
from its *Falling Place* to an ancient seafloor city.
Another cetacean carcase in a line-up of white stones
bleached bones rearing like cathedrals between hot
bubbling thermal vents or icy seeps where steel-
bending water pressure ruptures two great lungs
& stills a generous heart.
Hot volcano ranges peppered with black smokers spit
sulphur copper & rich metals where oxygen is absent
signalling a new party starter for
swallowers & gulpers snaggletooths & loosejaws
those nippers rippers & strippers that bump & grind
around this Beggar's Banquet
at *Ahab's Café de Whales.*

II

Down too far bumping through these hellish depths
evolutionary leftovers eke out their long days praying
for something with a shelf life to descend a cause
for celebration. Some light up their luminous red joy
flashing through the blackness. Others simply grope
about/along/around/ahead spelling out today's menu
in barnacles of Braille like medals worn across the dead
whale's skin. Start tearing into this new Moby Dick.
They are feasting now in these Hadian depths
devouring this fine new cachalot
resting in a gravy of rich ooze.
Opening up a noble carcass inhaling rich aromas of raw
flesh *Mmmm Mmmm* they sigh in bubbles stretching wide
mouths wider full of fearsome fangs steel traps iron grates
iron maidens that crush & smash & gnash spilling
sweet particles trailing sea-snot from rubbery lips
now these Abyssal halls are fully decked. *

III

How many fish will drum their fins on empty tables
if we bury stranded whales? Give them 'Christian' burials
by hiding them in sand dunes never letting them *fall*
as Mother Nature intended?
Stealing from royalty & beggars ignoring the seas' disabled
who stare at empty ocean beds & wonder if starvation is a
blessing or a curse where Life—that eternal punishment—
is a sentence to be served in total darkness.
Such banquets should go on for years and years *
until each carcass disappears noble spirits reabsorbed
by ill-assorted bits of species burning with a relentless
drive to survive & thrive where the light won't shine.
Some crawled from this primordial sea
while others stayed behind gnashing
their testbench teeth & waiting to evolve ...
please God!

* *One dead whale can feed these bottom dwellers for up to twenty-
seven years and various other micro-creatures for close to a century*

Towards Blue

Jan Dean

try the Yuelarbah track
    start before sunrise
        take a torch
            don't mind the winding
          trees give comfort with a sense of caress
      breathe in freshness
            believe this way is best
bird-choristers herald dawn
          at first light, from the waterfall and lagoon
mists rise, tinged-blue
      soon the sun breaks through the horizon
          sending slithers of sparkles
    that startle across the ocean
          embracing the shore and surrounds
with sprinkles of jewels, dependent
      on lives well-spent; sapphire, aquamarine
turquoise, lapis lazuli, intense and evolving
        yet over too soon, and before you know it
you have bathed in the bluest of blue, without getting wet

Debbie's Fairies

Mark Liston

At her open window she nods,
two blue eyes at two blue wrens
pecking pieces of morning sunshine.
The gardener scrapes leaves:
like loud alarms they scurry
under shrubs, like tiptoeing to safety—
mini bits of sky to rustle in fallen petals.

Though her wheelchair button blinks blue
flat bbbb … battery she shrugs,
I tuck in her dressing gown, *little chilly*
to visit the trees and banksia bushes.

But she stares under the shrubs
where the fff … fairies live, pointing again
perhaps to watch the way their tailfeathers
wave like fingers saying hello.
We roll close for Debbie to say *hello* back.

Intangible

Kathryn R Bennett

Sunrays scatter as they dance
In water and air
Delivering blues;

From cyan to indigo
The deeper they drown
Their colour-waves bruise;

Cerulean and midnight
Give names to their shades
The higher they cruise.

Nature's unpigmented gift
Demands attention,
Conjures sublime views,

Inspires artistic capture
Of evanescent
Intangible hues.

nuages

Kit Kelen

have you noticed how
sometimes a cloud comes together
              from nothing?
you fix on a patch of blue
          then it's not
it's like a story starts

afoot up there, doors everywhere
dense, fluffy
a bath overrun in the mirror

scud or single file
sometimes clouds compete to be
float like signs of mind
(soon forgot)

still something is shaping
here's tortoise, here's Achilles
really they're pictures of nothing

are they of this world at all?
once each had a name

have you ever noticed
how a cloud breaks up?
fix on it—dinosaur coasts
        arrows, fluff dragons
diagrams and gone until

the day comes still
then there's your patch of blue

Sensing Blue
Cedar Whelan

My friend has no sight. We talk about how she feels when people mention colours she's never seen. The coral of her coat, the teal of her boots. I imagine her world is perse all the time. But that's the speculation of a sighted person. People describe colours to her. Do they want her to know what she's missing? The green of the grass, the brown of her tea, the blue of the rain. It's for them, not for her. She accepts the knowing of not knowing.

My child has low visual acuity and no depth perception, depending on colour contrasts for meaning of all around them. I remember them at two, half their vocabulary the names of colours, more for blue than any other. At four, announcing the yellow bus leaving at the end of the block. Skipping backwards at five, saying they avoided obstacles using their fourth eye. Out of the mouths of babes.

I have 20:20 vision they say—for hindsight at least. I sit in the cobalt-trimmed white cottage between cyan ocean and azure sky merging at the horizon, phthalo pen in hand, and ponder the permutations of perception. There are times we just don't know what we don't know.

Blue Whale Wish

Anne Walsh

May every second be a leap year for you

into the oceans of the you you've always been.

Regardless of the you others tried to create

from the only parts of you they could see

from their too small boats.

There's no word for you

in their dry languages longing as they do

for the sea. Or for the depths you swim.

Their tears are salty because their tongues are bland

Manta Ray

Phillip M Williams

fin   tips
cut   the
aqua   marine
silky surface as she cruises carefree and
curious s c a n n i n g my alien body propelled
by one silent powerful swoop of triangular wings
horn - shaped lobes f u n n e l water into a
g a p i n g m o u t h as she glides by casting a
diamond-shaped shadow on the palette of
coral below I am m e s m e r i s e d
her stunning sleek skin
glistens e x q u i s i t e l y
in the pristine
P a c i f i c

~

~

b

l

u

e

www.ingramcontent.com/pod-product-compliance
Lightning Source LLC
Chambersburg PA
CBHW030417120726
47904CB00007B/2317